A Long, Long Time Ago...

Tales from the hills of India

Prithi Chand Thakur

Independently Published

ISBN-13: 9798431241970

Contents

True Disciple

A long, long time ago, a small village existed at the foothill of a great mountain. The people of that village were very simple and worship the mountain. Some believed that the peak of the mountain is closest to the heaven and other celestial bodies, and spirits of their ancestors reside there. The mountain was true paradise filled with lush green forests, cool mountain streams, and quiet meadows where butterflies flit above the wildflowers.

The streams that flowed down mountain's steep terrain fed the plants, animals, and gave the villagers all they needed for life. The mountain had treasure of medicinal herbs, flowers, timber and minerals which villagers used to harness for their benefits.

As time passed the people of village became selfish and greedy. They started over-exploiting the resources of mountain beyond their personal needs. This over-exploitation caused the withering of mountain and the birds, animals living in that mountain started to move from there. The mountain, which was majestic example of might and fertility, became a pitiful sight of barren rocks. As days passed and villagers' greed increased the mountain started turning black.

In that village was a poor young orphaned boy who lived with his old grandfather. For living, he used to tend the sheep of villagers, so he came to be known as *Fhuaal* (keeper of sheep). His grandfather used to tell him stories of the beauty of mountain.

"It was a part of paradise on earth. A very large area was covered with green fields. Fruit trees were abundant. The travelers meet the beautiful trees of apricots, plums, peaches and apples at the way-side. These trees were allowed to grow to enormous sizes without pruning. A splendid panorama of snowy peaks was presented in all directions. Several glaciers spread down from the mountain presenting a bewitching scene," the grandfather told.

One day, an old man who was selling *Sigles* (dumplings made from wheat) came to the village. He had white hair and a white beard and his clothing was very old and worn. He carried a heavy load of hot *Sigles* which looked and smelled deliciously good to eat. However, everyone in the village thought the old man was stupid because he yelled:

"Hot and delicious *Sigles*! One for five rupees, two for ten rupees and three for free!"

"Is he mad?" the villagers asked surprised.

"Hot and delicious *Sigles*! One for five rupees, two for ten rupees and three for free!" the crazy old man yelled again.

More and more villagers began to gather around. They whispered in low voices, "Can this be true? Three *Sigles* for free? Is this old man making fool of us or tricking us?"

"Who cares! I'll eat three *Sigles* first and see whether it's free or not," a young man said.

"Mmmm, these *Sigles* are so good!" the young man said while he was eating the *Sigles*. The old man's *Sigles* were as big as apple. When the young man finished his second *Sigle*, he was so full that he could not eat anymore. However, he asked the old man, "If I eat three *Sigles*, you'll not ask for a single paisa, right?"

"Absolutely right, I never tell lies. I already said three for free," the old man replied.

The young man stuffed down another *Sigle* just so he could have the all for free. The old man kept his word and didn't charge from him any money.

The other villagers began to order the old man's delicacy. Everyone ordered three free *Sigles*; no one ordered either one or two. After a while, the load of old man was all eaten by the villagers.

"You all do have a good appetite folks," the old man said smilingly.

People who did not get any *Sigle* watched the old man leave with disappointment.

A villager who just ate three *Sigles* cried out suddenly, "Look! How is it that the mountain behind the village is looking darker than usual?"

"Stop talking nonsense! You ate too many *Sigles* which has made your mind confused," someone replied.

The villagers began to talk about the old man. "Ha! I can't believe there is a stupid person who would sell three *Sigles* for free."

"His *Sigles* are so delicious. I wonder what they're made of, and where this old man came from? I wish he could come every day," thought everyone.

On the second day, the crazy old man came to the village again. He yelled, "Hot and delicious *Sigles*! One for five rupees, two for ten rupees and three for free!" Everyone left what they were doing and began to gather around the old man. They started fighting each other to reach near the old man. They ate the *Sigles* so fast that they didn't even chew on them. After a while, the load was all eaten again.

On the third day, the same thing happened; villagers were trying to eat as much as they possibly could. Suddenly, a voice was heard:

"Old man! Can you please give me one *Sigle*?"

Everyone was surprised. They turned and stared at our little boy Fhuaal who asked the old man sincerely.

"Kid, did you hear me clearly? One for five rupees, two for ten rupees and three for free. Why do you want just one *Sigle* when you could get three for free?"

"I know," the young boy replied, "but I see how you carried a heavy load of *Sigles* everyday and not made any money. I feel sorry for you. I really want to help, but I have only enough money to pay for one *Sigle*."

Every one of the greedy villagers felt ashamed when they heard the young kid's words.

"Don't worry about me kid," said the old man, "here take these three *Sigles* and you need not to pay any money to me."

"No, I insist, you'll have to take money, and give me only one *Sigle*," the kid replied.

"You're very kind son! I've found you at last. You are the kind of person suitable to be my pupil. I am the mountain god."

Everyone realized now that the old man was actually the mountain god. To find himself a trustworthy and kindhearted pupil, the mountain god had disguised himself as a senile old man in order to test the people's hearts. His *Sigles* were not real, but were made from dung.

After the villagers heard the mountain god's explanation, they ran to see the leftover *Sigles*. However, all they could see was a pot full of dung. When they turned and looked at the mountain, the villagers saw the mountain is not dark any more.

The mountain god took the young man back to his place and prepared to teach this kindhearted boy all his magic.

As for the villagers, they felt really disgusted about eating all the dung and wished they could vomit out all the dung they had eaten. They regretted their actions and blamed themselves for being greedy.

It is said in hilly countryside that deities' powers are replenished by the devotion of their worshippers. The more genuine the devotion will be the more powerful a deity will be. And only a kind-hearted person can be a true devotee.

The Selfless Hunter

A long time ago, a hunter named Meghu lived in a hill village with his wife Tara and daughter Naina. During winters the whole village gets covered in heavy snow. So every family used to gather enough wood and food in the summer and store them to be used in the snowy winters.

The hunter's family also did the same. But unexpectedly, some guests, who were traveling through their village, visit them. They stayed in their house for some days because all roads were closed due to heavy snowfall. Since Meghu's family had stocked food and meat for themselves only, their stock soon got depleted and caused scarcity of food in their house.

One day when the food stock was nearly exhausted, Meghu decided to go out to jungle for the hunt. Tara gave him three *rotis* to eat during the day.

"I don't need *rotis*," said Meghu, "these are last three *rotis* left with us, please save them for yourself and Naina!"

But Tara pleaded and requested him to take *rotis* with him. With heavy heart he kept *rotis* in his coat and said goodbye to his family.

He treaded whole noon but couldn't find a single animal or bird. In winters animals either hibernate or migrate to warmer plains and there were no animals on hills. Meghu became very disappointed. After walking a few more miles he came across a mountain cave. He saw a Buddhist monk standing near the mouth of cave. The monk told him that he was in meditation from last two months and had just came out of the cave. Since he hadn't eaten from last two months he is very hungry now. Hearing this Meghu offered him the *rotis* his wife had given him. The monk accepted only one *roti* and returned the rest two to Meghu to take home for his daughter and wife.

"Have you seen any animal nearby?" Meghu asked.

"You'll not find any animal here at this time of year," monk said, "but you should hurry back to home as a snowstorm is approaching this way."

After bidding farewell to monk, Meghu set to return home with heavy heart. He was worried that how he and his family will spend the rest of winters without food.

He knocked at the door and his wife opened the door with a smiling face.

"Hey, you look tired," said Tara, "please sit down and I'll bring hot water to wash your face and feet."

"Yeah, but…," he did not had the courage to tell his wife that he had returned empty handed.

Tara brought warm water and said, "Now, tell me, where is the treasure that you brought for us?"

"Treasure… what treasure are you talking Tara?" he said angrily as he thought his wife is taunting him for returning without any kill.

"Now come on, do not be so rude, we know you are trying to befool us, you have treasure for me and our daughter!"

And then the daughter came running out and said, "Father, give us the treasure and in return we have a surprise for you too!"

"Surprise for me?" said the hunter.

"Yes, mother has made *rotis* and deer meat for us," said Naina.

"What?" Meghu was stunned, "where did you get the flour and deer?"

"Ha ha ha ha… you're trying to fool us, right father? One man came with a big deer and flour and told that you were going uphill for a treasure hunt and had sent the 'kill' to us… now come on show what treasure have you brought for us!" Tara said.

Meghu said nothing. He opened the buttons of his coat and went into the room, thanking in his thoughts the monk for the miracle. He knew it's the monk who had done all this for his family.

Meanwhile, the daughter and the wife checked the pockets of the coat and shouted in joy seeing the two necklaces in the pocket having gold beads in them.

Now the hunter realized that the two *rotis* which monk had returned have actually turned into gold-beaded necklaces.

So that is how the selfless hunter got rewarded for his good deeds.

From that day on, the people of the region are keeping food grains, dry woods etc. near the caves so that monks and the traveling disciples may eat them and bless the people too.

The Mirror

A long, long time ago in a shanty hill village there lived a man and his wife. They had a beautiful little daughter Maya. She was the joy and pride of her parents, and they loved her very much. The man was a wood sculpturist and used to go deep into the jungle to search fine woods. Their life was very enjoyable and they were very happy with it.

One day a messenger from king visited their home and informed that king is looking for a fine craftsman to sculpture the idol of goddess from wood, and the father had to go to city with the messenger. Hearing this there was much excitement in the home. In those days, there were no means of transportations in hills so they had to travel on foot hundreds of miles.

The wife was very anxious as she helped to pack things of her husband and get him ready for the long journey. She wished that she could accompany him, but the distance was too great for the mother and daughter to go, and besides that, she has to take care of the home.

When everything was ready at last, the husband stood in the foyer waving goodbye to his wife and daughter.

"Don't worry about me, I will come back soon," he said. "While I am away take care of yourself and Maya."

"Yes! We shall be all right, but you must take care of yourself and come back as soon as possible," said the wife with tears in her eyes.

The little Maya was the only one to smile, for she was ignorant of the sorrow of parting, and did not know that going to the capital was at all different from walking to the near jungle, which her father did very often. She ran to his side, and caught hold of his long sleeve of coat.

"Father, I will behave very nice, so please bring me a doll when you will come back," Maya said.

As the father turned to take a last look at his little family, he felt as if his heart is sinking, so hard was it for him to leave them behind, for they had never been separated before for such a long time. But he knew that he must go, for the call was imperative. With a great effort he ceased to think, and resolutely turning away he went quickly down the hill with messenger. His wife, holding up the child in her arms watched him as he went between the thick pines till he was lost in the haze of the distance.

"Now father has gone, so you and I must take care of everything till he comes back," said the mother.

"Ok Ma, I will be very good," said Maya, "and when the father will come home I'll play with my doll."

"Sure my angel! You must pray for a safe journey to your father till he comes back."

"Oh, yes, when he comes home again how happy I shall be," said the child, clapping her hands, and her face growing bright with joy at the glad thought.

Many weeks passed, and the day came when husband returned home. He had traveled many days, and was all tired up with heavy beard on his face, but his wife and child knew him at a glance, and flew to meet him from either side, each catching hold of one of his sleeves in their eager greeting.

As soon as they had sat down, the father opened a wooden basket that he had brought in with him, and took out a beautiful doll.

"Here," he said to the little girl, "is a present for you. It is a prize for taking care of mother and the house so well while I was away."

"Thank you," said the child rejoicing, and then put out her little hands to take the doll. The doll was prettier than anything she had ever seen. She was very delighted and her face sparked with joy, and she had no eyes and no thought for anything else. She quickly ran out of her house to show her doll to her friends.

Then the husband took out a shiny little thing from the box, and gave it to his wife, and said:

"And this is for you."

The wife took the shining object, which had a small handle attached to it. One side of the object was very bright, and the other was covered with smoothly carved wood. She had never seen such a thing in her life. She gazed into the shining object, and looking up with surprise and wonder pictured on her face, she said:

"Who is this looking at me in this round thing? What is it that you have given to me?"

The husband laughed and said:

"It is your own beautiful face that you see my dear. What I have brought you is called a *mirror*, and whoever looks into its clear surface can see their own face reflected there."

Poor wife has only seen her reflection in the water and never ever thought that there can be any such thing where one can see their reflection so clearly.

"The king gave me this mirror as a prize for my good work. The mirror represents the soul of who look into it, and if the mirror is clean so your soul will also be clean. So you must take great care of this mirror, and use it carefully," husband said.

"I shall certainly treasure it as a valuable possession, and never will I use it carelessly." Saying so, she lifted it as high as her forehead, in grateful acknowledgment of the gift, and then shut it up in its box and put it away.

Time passed away in the peaceful home, and the parents saw their fondest hopes realized as their daughter grew from childhood into a beautiful girl of sixteen. She grew as beautiful as her mother was in her youth.

But as the happiness is part of the life so are the sorrows. One day the mother was taken ill. First the father and daughter thought that it was only a minor cold, and were not particularly anxious. But the days went by and mother's condition worsens. Without proper healthcare facilities in those days in hills, the poor woman grew weaker day by day. The father and daughter were stricken with grief, and day or night Maya never left her mother's side.

One day mother asked Maya to come closer to her. Maya sat near her mother's bed, the mother roused herself and taking her daughter's hand said:

"Maya, I am sure that nothing can save me now. When I am dead, promise me to take care of your dear father and to try to be a good and dutiful daughter."

"Oh, mother," said the girl as the tears rushed to her eyes, "please don't say like this. You'll be well and healthy soon."

"Daughter, I have something to give you whereby to remember me when I am gone," said mother.

Putting her hand out, she took from the side of the pillow a square wooden box. Undoing this very carefully, she took out the mirror that her husband had given her years ago.

"When you were a little child your father went up to the city and brought me back this treasure; it is called a *mirror*. I want you to have this. If you are lonely and long to see me sometimes, then take out this mirror and in the clear and shining surface you will always see me, and though I shall not be able to speak, I shall understand and sympathize with you, whatever may happen to you in the future." With these words the dying woman handed the mirror to her daughter.

Thus said, the mother left for heavenly abode.

The bereaved father and daughter were wild with grief, and they abandoned themselves to their bitter sorrow.

Maya's love for her dead mother did not grow less with time, and so keen was her remembrance, that everything in daily life reminded her of her mother. She immersed herself completely into the household chores and helping her father. As time passed Maya completely forgot about the mirror.

A year spent in mourning had thus passed away when, by the advice of his relatives, the father married again, and the daughter now found herself under the authority of a step-mother.

Step-mothers are proverbial all the world over, and this one's heart was not as her first smiles were. As the days and weeks grew into months, the step-mother began to treat the motherless girl unkindly and to try and come between the father and the child.

Sometimes she went to her husband and complained of her step-daughter's behavior, but the father knowing that this was to be expected, took no notice of her ill-natured complaints. Instead of lessening his affection for his daughter, as the woman desired, her grumblings only made him think of her the more. The woman soon saw that he began to show more concern for his lonely child than before. This did not please her at all, and she began to turn over in her mind how she could, by some means or other, drive her step-child out of the house.

Maya was the one who was suffering most. On the one hand, she had to bear the hatred of step-mother, and on the other hand she was not able to share her feelings with her father anymore.

One day when her father was out, and Maya was immersed in her mother's memories, she remembered the box her mother had given her. She took out the box that contained the mirror, her heart beating with expectation as she lifted the mirror out and gazed into its smooth face.

Behold, her mother's words were true! In the round mirror before her she saw her mother's face; but, oh, the joyful surprise! It was not her mother thin and wasted by illness, but the young and beautiful woman as she remembered her far back in the days of her own earliest childhood. It seemed to the girl that the face in the mirror must soon speak, almost that she heard the voice of her mother telling her again to grow up a good woman and a dutiful daughter, so earnestly did the eyes in the mirror look back into her own.

"It is certainly my mother's soul that I see. She knows how miserable I am without her and she has come to comfort me. Whenever I long to see her she will meet me here; how grateful I ought to be!" thought Maya.

And from this time the weight of sorrow was greatly lightened for her young heart. Every morning, to gather strength for the day's duties before her, and every evening, for consolation before she lay down to sleep, did the young girl take out the mirror and gaze at the reflection which in the simplicity of her innocent heart she believed to be her mother's soul. Daily she grew in the likeness of her dead mother's character, and was gentle and kind to all, and a dutiful daughter to her father.

One day the step-mother grew suspicious of Maya's activities and whispers coming from her room. She peeped into her room in the early morning, and saw a human reflection in an object which Maya had held in her hands. She became frightened at what she had seen. She was convinced that Maya has made an image of her and is trying to kill her by black magic art, cursing her daily.

She decided to know the complete truth and one day she sent Maya out of the house to run some errands, and sneaked into her room. She took out the wooden box from under the pillow and opened it. She held the mirror in her hands and saw her reflection in it. Now she was sure that Maya has imprisoned her soul in the mirror. She was so frightened that the mirror dropped from her hands and shattered into pieces. Now there were many reflections on the floor, and woman became more frightened that her soul has now shattered into many pieces.

This superstition set so deep in her heart that she fell sick, and with passing time her condition started deteriorating. Maya being a dutiful daughter tended her step-mother dedicatedly. In the meantime her father had to go to city again on the call of the king. He asked Maya to take care of her ailing step-mother.

Maya tried by amiability and obedience to show her goodwill and to mollify her step-mother, and to break down that wall of prejudice and misunderstanding that she knew generally stood between step-parents and their step-children. The step-mother never trusted her, but somewhere in her heart she was moved by the dedication and services of Maya. She also stopped nagging and scolding Maya because she believed that only Maya can bring her broken soul back. Maya was surprised by this change in behavior of her step-mother, and she also started liking her. She left no stone unturned in making her step-mother feel comfortable. Thus the days passed and tending her sick step-mother, Maya forgot about the mirror.

The day came when her father returned from his journey. He has brought the similar mirror this time also for her wife. Wife looked into the mirror and rejoiced to see that her soul is complete again. She said:

"Oh dear husband! You've completed my soul, now please tell Maya to release my soul from this object."

He couldn't understand what her wife is saying, and why she is blaming Maya and what for. Maya was also stunned to hear her step-mother's accusations.

"What are you talking about?" he asked.

"Maya is a good girl, I know, and she has cared me a lot when you were away. But she has been overpowered by some evil forces which made her imprisoned my soul in this object."

Husband remembered having noticed that his daughter stayed much in her room of late and kept herself away from everyone, even when visitors came to the house. Putting this fact together with his wife's alarm, he thought that there might be something to account for the strange story.

"Maya, is it really true? Have you forgotten what I told you, that although she is your step-mother you must be obedient and loyal to her? What evil spirit has taken possession of your heart that you should be so wicked?"

And the father's eyes filled with sudden tears to think that he should have to upbraid his daughter in this way.

She on her part did not know what he meant, for she had never heard of the superstition that by praying over an image it is possible to cause the death of a hated person. But she saw that she must speak and clear herself somehow. She loved her father dearly, and could not bear the idea of his anger. She put out her hand on his knee deprecatingly:

"Father! father! do not say such dreadful things to me. I am still your obedient child. I should never be able to curse anyone who belonged to you, much less pray for the death of one you love."

Then she told him of her mother's last words, and of how she had promised to meet her child whenever she looked into the mirror. But still the father could not understand the simplicity of his daughter's character in not knowing that what she saw reflected in the mirror was in reality her own face, and not that of her mother.

"What do you mean?" he asked. "I do not understand how you can meet the soul of your dead mother by looking in this mirror?"

"It is indeed true," said the girl, "and if you don't believe what I say, look for yourself," and she took the mirror from her step-mother's hand and placed the mirror before her. There, looking back from the smooth metal disk, was her own sweet face. She pointed to the reflection seriously:

"Do you doubt me still?" she asked earnestly, looking up into his face.

With an exclamation of sudden understanding the father smote his two hands together.

"How stupid I am! At last I understand. Your face is as like your mother's thus you have looked at the reflection of your face all this time, thinking that you were brought face to face with your dead mother! This is a mirror, and whoever looks in it sees his own reflection."

The step-mother, who was hearing all this felt very guilty and stupid. She broke down and said:

"I am ashamed! I am ashamed! You have been such a wonderful daughter to me. Through no fault of yours, but with a step-mother's jealous heart, I have disliked you all the time. When I saw you gaze daily into the mirror for long intervals, I concluded that you had found out how I disliked you, and that you were out of revenge trying to take my life by magic art. I shall never forget the wrong I have done you in so misjudging you, and in causing your father to suspect you. From this day I throw away my old and wicked heart, and in its place I put a new one, clean and full of repentance. I shall think of you as a child that I have borne myself. I shall love and cherish you with all my heart, and thus try to make up for all the unhappiness I have caused you. Please forgive me and accept me as your mother."

Thus did the unkind step-mother humble herself and ask forgiveness of the girl she had so wronged. Such was the sweetness of the girl's disposition that she willingly forgave her step-mother, and never bore a moment's resentment or malice towards her afterwards. The father saw by his wife's face that she was truly sorry for the past, and was greatly relieved to see the terrible misunderstanding wiped out of remembrance by both the wrong-doer and the wronged.

From this time on, the three lived together happily. No such trouble ever darkened the home again, and the young girl gradually forgot that year of unhappiness in the tender love and care that her step-mother now bestowed on her. Her patience and goodness were rewarded at last.

Dirty Pig

Lying at the foot of the Himalayas, there was a great forest. All trees and bushes of that forest were very lush and green. The forest had rolling hill peaks and in the distance had the high snow covered peaks.

The forest was home of numerous kinds of animals, such as tiger, yaks, leopards, bears, musk deer, rabbits, wild buffalo, wild pigs etc. The tiger was the king and all the other animals were his subjects and lived in fear of him.

But the tiger was rather a good king. He never killed any animal except to satisfy his hunger occasionally. When he had full stomach he was generally sluggard and used to wander leisurely throughout the forest. He even nodded at the other animals and took their greetings as they met him on the way.

One day the tiger killed a fully grown deer, and ate until his belly was ready to burst. When his meal was over, he went to a nearby lake to quench his thirst. As it happened, a rotund and zestful young pig had also come to the same lake to drink water. The pig watched the tiger and it gave him the jitters. He hid behind a tree, held his breath and stood perfectly still, hoping that the tiger would not see him.

But the tiger had already seen him, and he had no intentions to catch the pig or to kill him. And it would have been difficult for him to run after the pig at all, as he was already full to the brim. The tiger drank water quietly, ignoring the pig. Tiger thought that he is getting old and if he'll frighten the pig it will not come to the lake again, which was the easiest place to catch the prey, and it may also warn the other animals to stay away from lake. Keeping this in mind, the tiger slowly walked away, feigning that he is feeling sleepy and had not seen the pig at all.

When the sight of tiger was lost in the dense bushes, the pig heaved a sigh of relief. His heart started beating again and the blood restarted flowing through his body.

"Did the tiger saw me?", he thought.

He concluded that the tiger did saw him and went away quietly because he was frightened of him.

"The tiger is no more suitable to be a king. He must vacate the post. Rather it is the he who should be the king of the forest," the pig thought.

At the very thought of becoming the king of forest and having so many subjects, the pig strutted to the edge of the lake and called out to the tiger, calling him names and challenging him. An old owl who came there hearing the shouting of pig said:

"Are you insane? Why are you calling names to the king of forest?"

"He is a puny king, and he is no match to me. I'll challenge him for a duel and all animals of forest will see that I'm more powerful and worthy king," the pig grunted loudly.

The tiger, who was not even able to stand properly, did not come charging after the pig, and said:

"If you wish so, then come after two days at the same place. I accept your challenge."

The pig readily agreed, and feeling very pleased with himself, he returned back to his friends in the forest. They all enquired about the reason for his happiness. The pig raised his curly tail in pride and said:

"You should treat me with more respect now, as I'm the future king of forest."

His friends started laughing at him.

"May be he slipped on the sloppy banks of lake, and hurt his head," one old pig said.

All animals laughed heartedly again, and at this the pig related them the entire story. All his friends were gaping at him with eyes as big as plates. They could not believe that the pig had courage to challenge the tiger.

"He definitely has lost his mind," said the old pig again, "may be the tiger was not hungry and that is why he had let the pig go. Otherwise he would have devoured him."

When all his friends said the same thing, the pig realized that they could be right. Now he began to shake with fright. He was regretting his decision of challenging the tiger. He decided not to go to the lake after two days, and spend the whole week hiding in his house. But other pigs did not agree.

"If the tiger did not find you at the lake at the given day then he will declare war on us pigs," one pig said.

"Yes, he will attack our place and hunt each pig down and kill them," said another.

"You'd stirred the hornet's nest so only you must face the consequences," they all said in one voice.

Hearing his friends, the young pig was scared out of his wits. He asked them for help. His friends suggested him to go to the eldest wise pig.

The young pig wasted no time, and went running to wise pig and told him the whole story. After hearing the whole story patiently the wise pig rebuked the young pig for his stupidity. The young pig cried and pleaded the wise pig to help him and save his life. The wise pig took pity on him and asked for one night to think over it.

That night the young pig couldn't sleep and kept thinking about the whole episode and cursing himself. Next morning he and all other pigs rushed to the place of wise pig. The wise pig was lost in thoughts and after some time he looked up and said:

"There is only one way by which the tiger may spare your life."

The pig started dancing around for sheer joy and said, "I'll do anything, if it can save my life."

"Before you go to the tiger you must make yourself as dirty as possible, and eat filth so that nobody could even breathe near you," said the wise pig.

The young pig jumped at the idea. Just before his duel with

the tiger he rolled in mud and slush, dried himself out and rolled again and yet again, and ate lot of filth. When he finally reached the lake he didn't look like a pig at all. He was one big ball of mud and soil, and many flies were buzzing around him.

The tiger was already there, waiting for his meal to appear. But when he saw the lump of mud before him he was taken aback. He was shocked to see the pig so dirty. The young pig introduced himself and said that it is him whom the tiger was supposed to fight. The tiger looked at this walking filth and wrinkled his nose in repugnance. Gone were his dreams of a clean, delicious soft meal of pig meat! Now all he wanted was to get rid of this filthy creature before him. He roared at the pig and asked him to disappear, and never to cross his path again.

The young pig managed to get away, though his body was trembling with fear. He ran as fast as he could and didn't even look back once. He rushed to the wise pig and thanked him with all his heart. After that all the pigs decided that in future they would remain as dirty as possible, so the predator would not be tempted to eat them. And that is why, to this day, pigs like to loll about in mud and eat filth.

Parrot Prince and Debu

A poor farmer had three sons and a daughter. The family had a small landholding where they'd grown an orchard of apple trees. One morning when the family woke up, they saw that branches of many apple trees were lying broken and numerous fruits, half eaten, were scattered on the ground. The farmer ordered his sons to catch the culprit and assigned the elder son to guard the orchard at night. While guarding the orchard the elder son lie down on hay for rest but soon fell asleep. In the morning many trees were again ruined. He lied to his father that he was awake all night, but didn't saw anyone.

Next day the old man assigned his second son to guard the orchard. But he also fell asleep and the result was same. The youngest son, Debu, was a simpleton and lazy, but as there was no one else to rely on the farmer sent him to guard the orchard. Debu took a net with himself to the field at night, and hid himself in hay heap.

Later just after midnight he heard a squawking and fluttering noise. He popped his head from hay and saw that an extremely beautiful and big parrot was flying from one tree to another. He was eating apples with his big, sharp, iron-like beak, and after eating a little littering rest of apple on the ground. The parrot was magnificent looking; his feathers were of golden colors, his claws were strong and sharp like steel, and when he flies a strong wind blows. Debu decided to catch it and when the parrot was busy in eating apple he threw the net and trapped it.

"Please let me go!", begged the parrot.

"Hey... you can talk?", Debu was surprised.

"Yes! I'm a god prince, but I was very naughty and talkative, so to punish me my father turned me into a parrot with a spell and asked to spend some time on earth. I can grant you three wishes if you'll free me! Anytime you need me, just say *'Come-come O' heavenly bird and sit on my hand, fulfill my wish by waving your magic wand!'*. I'll appear immediately and will fulfill your wish."

Debu let the parrot go but first took his word never to ruin their orchard again. When Debu returned home in the morning, his brothers asked, "Did you saw the thief?"

"Yes, I saw a golden parrot!", he replied.

His brothers laughed; however, nobody vandalized the orchard since then.

One day a royal messenger visited their village announcing that the king has decided to find a suitable husband for the princess.

"Come, young men, to the festival at the main market. The king has decided to marry his daughter and he is looking for a suitor," he announced.

The people were amazed to hear this announcement as everybody knows that king loved his daughter very much, in fact so much that he did not wish her to marry, so he had built a secret house under the ground for her, and there he kept her away hidden from all.

It was a surprising announcement for all, so the older brothers prepared and went to the festival, but didn't took the youngest Debu with them. Debu decided to go to main market by himself. He picked a basket and set out from his house.

"Where are you going?" asked her sister.

"I'm going to pick mushrooms in jungle for food," replied Debu.

Then he reached the orchard. When he was assured that nobody is looking him he said:

"Come-come O' heavenly bird and sit on my hand, fulfill my wish by waving your magic wand!"

Suddenly a bright light flashed and there appear the parrot.

"Why have you summoned me O kind Debu?" asked the parrot.

"King is looking a suitor for princess, and I want to go there too. Can you change my appearance and take me there?" asked Debu.

"Here", the parrot plucked a feather and gave to Debu, "keep this feather on your head", said the parrot.

Debu took the feather and put it on his head. Suddenly a light flashed and Debu saw that he has been changed into a handsome man as can't be imagined or described, and his rugged clothes converted to silk dress.

"Remember, your this appearance will remain only till the sunset, so don't forget to return the orchard by that time," warned the parrot.

Then Debu followed the flying parrot who led him to the main market. There were hundreds of people in the market, and king was sitting on a palanquin, and next was seated the beautiful princess. Such was her beauty that Debu even forgot to blink his eyes.

A long pole was erected in the middle of market. The pole was so high that its top end was touching the clouds.

King announced, "At the top of this pole is tied the royal ring, whoever will bring this ring down I'll bestow him my daughter."

There was a long queue of suitors who were trying every means to bring down the ring. Some were shooting arrows, some were throwing stones, and some were shaking the pole, but nobody succeeded. Debu tried his best to reach near the pole, but the crowd was so heavy that poor soul nearly got trampled under their feet. When the sun was about to set Debu decided to return home. He quickly reached the orchard where he again became the normal Debu. He quickly picked his basket and randomly picked some mushrooms and went home.

"Where have you picked these rotten mushrooms," asked his sister, "who will eat them, you're such a fool?"

Debu didn't say anything and waited till his brothers returned. They described the unknown handsome man to their father and sister. The next day older brothers went to the main market again, and Debu took the basket, went to the orchard and shouted:

"Come-come O' heavenly bird and sit on my hand, fulfill my wish by waving your magic wand!"

In a moment the parrot appeared, and Debu asked him for the same thing. Then Debu reached the market, but today also the crowd was so huge that it was not possible for him to even reach near the pole. Debu decided to take the parrot's help this time. He found a secluded place in market and summoned the parrot, and ask his help to bring down the royal ring.

"Are you sure that you want to do this, remember it'll be your last wish that I can grant," said the parrot.

"Yes," replied Debu.

He brings the parrot near the pole and the bird flied toward the top of pole. Everyone was looking in awe when the parrot brought the ring back in his iron beak. When he put the ring on Debu's palm it got pricked from his iron beak. Blood started oozing from his hand, Debu panicked and ran back to his home. "Catch him! Catch him!" shouted the crowd but there was no trace of Debu.

He returned to orchard where his appearance changed back to normal. He wrapped a rag to his hand and hid the ring in it. When he returned home his brother saw the bandaged in his hand. "What is it," asked the brothers. "I was searching for mushrooms but grabbed a thorn," replied Debu.

The next day royal messenger again came to their village and announced that king is giving a feast in honor of his daughter. All young men have to come and those who will not come will be executed. So, next day all three brothers went to the feast.

Hundreds of people were sitting at the market, eating, drinking, and talking. At the end, the king went on to distribute gifts to all people from his own hands. When he reached near Debu, he saw the poor has a dress with holes, was all sooty himself, hair stands on end, and hand wrapped in a rag.

"What's wrong with your hand?" asked king, "go on, unwrap it!"

Debu unwrapped the rag, and everyone's eyes shone upon. Then king called his soldiers and asked them to take Debu out of his kingdom. Before soldiers could take him out Debu said, "You may hide your treasure, but it will be spent at last". Then soldiers dragged him out. His brothers were so terrorized that they couldn't muster courage to save their brother.

The boy wandered far and long, till at last he reached deep in the jungles. He met a beautiful prince in the jungle. Prince said, "Didn't you recognize me, I'm the same parrot who helped you. My father was so happy for helping you that he frees me from curse. Now I'm here to help you one last time."

The god prince gave Debu princely clothing, a royal carriage, and a music box that could play many melodious tunes, and told him what to do. Debu returned to the kingdom, riding in his carriage and drove around for a while, till he met a boy. He gave the music box to the boy with some money and told him to play it everywhere but if anybody wishes to buy it report to me. The boy got into the carriage and took the music box with him. Soon the king saw the beautiful carriage and heard the sweet music of the music box. The king asked the boy who the owner was, and wished to buy the carriage and music box. The boy told the king that he must tell his employer, and he went back to Debu. He sent the carriage and the music box to the king for a present. The king was much pleased, for he knew the princess would be delighted, so he had the carriage and the music box taken to her, and played on the music box a long time. After king had gone, out stepped Debu from a secret compartment of the carriage, and knelt before the princess telling his love in gentle tones, and how he won the royal ring. She listened to him, much frightened at first, but later more composedly, till at last she gave him her heart and promised him her hand.

When the king came in again he found them sitting holding each other's hands. He demanded in a loud voice, "Who are you? How did you come here?" To this the boy modestly replied, saying that he had come concealed in the carriage, and told the king that "You may hide your treasure, but it will be spent at last." The king realized his mistake and beg sorry from Debu. Finally the king gave his consent to their marriage, and they lived happily ever after.

The Best Friend

In a serene remote hill village there lived a beautiful girl Sona with her father. She was very beautiful and dutiful to her father. She was married to a handsome young man of a distant village, when they were small children. As per tradition, bride stays at her natal home till she turns eighteen. Marriage is considered till then only as a ritual union and conjugal life begins only after a coming of age ceremony. After this ceremony, girl goes to live with her groom at his house.

When Sona turned eighteen, as per tradition, an auspicious day for her ceremony was announced by the village priest. The announcement brought mixed emotions in the house. On the one hand, young Sona was enlivened with the thoughts of starting a new life with her husband, and on the other hand, she was sad to leave her aging father alone by himself. Her father was also very sad because it was young Sona's delightful squeals which had filled the void of her life after his wife's death.

One day, as per her routine, Sona went to a stream to fetch water. It was lovely afternoon and sun rays were filtering through the needle like leaves of pines. The birds were chirping and at a distance she could hear the song of *pihu* (a humming bird).

Lost in her dreams about her future life, Sona sat for rest under a tree. A cool breeze was blowing and she gradually felt asleep there. When she opened her eyes, she found a little female hound lying down beside her. It seemed to be very much exhausted and starving because its ribs stood out on its body. It looked up at her eyes with its tired look.

"Where do you come from? Didn't you eat anything?" she asked the hound but it made no answer.

"Come with me, I'll feed you." Sona took the hound up in her one arm and carried the pitcher of water in other and set to return home.

At home Sona fed the hound, which she named *Chhaya* (because of its dusky color and habit of following Sona everywhere), and decided to keep it with her. Sona hadn't any friend left because all her friends had had their coming of age ceremony and they all were at their spouse's place.

"You're now my best friend," said Sona lovingly to Chhaya.

Sona decided to take Chhaya with her to her husband's place because that was new place to her and nobody was known to her there.

Finally the day came when Sona had to leave for her husband's home. On that day, relatives of groom's family came to take Sona along with them. With heavy heart her father decorated Sona's palanquin with bright and colorful flowers, and with moist eyes bid farewell to her sweet daughter. Riding on the palanquin, sobbing Sona was on the way to her new home. She was already missing her father's home where she spent the joyful moments of her adolescent. She recalled her puerile games which she played with her friends. It seemed to her that the mountain, streams, trees and birds all are saying goodbye to her. She almost cried of thoughts that she might not be able to see all these things in same form again in her life. Therefore, she gradually got into a sorrowful mood.

It was almost dark when they reached the village of groom. After customary ceremonies Sona retired for the day. Sona's new family was very loving and caring and she mixed in the family like sugar in the tea. Thus the days passed peacefully.

Sona always treated Chhaya with loving care and fed it well so that Chhaya grew up and bore four cute puppies. Sona always spent her time playing with the puppies or helping her mother-in-law in the kitchen. But as it happened, every time when Sona took off the lid of a rice-cooker off to serve rice to her family, Chhaya got the habit of sitting down in the kitchen to keep a watch.

One day, when Sona was about to take off the lid of the rice cooker, Chhaya suddenly stood up and leaped and ran over the rice-cooker again and again. Sona was surprised to see this. Chhaya had never behaved like this before. Soon Sona got irritated and said:

"What are you doing Chhaya? Stop it or I'll hit you with ladle!"

When Sona lifted up the ladle to warn Chhaya against doing that, it stopped. But after sometime, Chhaya leaped again when Sona put the ladle down. Sona thought that Chhaya was just trying to get playful and wish to attract her attention, but Chhaya didn't stop and repeated the same thing on the next day.

Soon Sona noticed that since the start of this behavior, some kind of allergic reaction is developing on the back of Chhaya. Sona thought that may be Chhaya got infected with mites, so she washed Chhaya well. But Chhaya's behavior didn't change and it even started spending her all time in the kitchen.

At this, Sona's husband got angry and said, "What an ungrateful dog it is! I'll kill it next morning."

That night, Sona's father-in-law invited a *sadhu*, who was passing through their village, to stay at their home for a night. The *sadhu* had mysterious power to understand the language of animals.

After dinner, when *sadhu* was cleansing himself near the verandah, he heard Chhaya's voices talking to her pups.

"Tonight is the last time to give you my breast. Suck as much as possible from my breast, my children."

"Why, ma?" asked one pup.

"Our owner will kill me next morning," said Chhaya.

"Why is that?" asked another pup.

"Alas! If only I could speak human language, I would tell them that a poisonous snake is living in the roof of kitchen and it is trying to poison our owner's meal from above whenever the lid was taken off. I always jumped and tried to prevent the poison from falling on the rice from above. But they couldn't make out what I was trying to do and are going to kill me," said Chhaya.

The *sadhu* looked at Chhaya's back, and found the dreadful condition of her poisoned back. Her hair was almost gone and her skin was badly blistered.

Then, the *sadhu* told the whole story to Sona's family. They immediately broke the roof and found a poisonous snake, which might have moved here recently. They killed the snake with a shovel.

After that day, the whole family treated Chhaya very well. Chhaya indeed proved itself to be the 'best friend' of Sona and lived long together with her.

Imla and Bimla

Once upon in ancient times at Karsog valley of Himachal, there lived many tribes of people in a peaceful environment. One tribal chief of these natives had two beautiful daughters. The elder one was called Imla and the younger one Bimla. They were very buoyant and spirited girls and liked to sing and dance. Especially, in spring season when it came the night of full moon, they always invite their friends, young girls of the same age, with them to go to the woods to sing and dance on the natural turf there. They looked very much like little lovely fairies bathed in the moonlight.

Almost all native people living in valley were peaceful and friendly except one tribe's chief named Mohar. He was vicious and cruel and often took advantage of others. He was physically very strong, so strong that he was capable of killing a leopard with his bare hands. Everybody, though disliking him, was afraid of him. He made people to call himself "the Lion of Karsog".

Once Mohar was in jungle hunting with two of his adjutants. They heard some cheerful singing in the woods. Following the music, they came upon Imla and Bimla with a group of young damsels happily singing and dancing swiftly on the green grass of meadows.

Mohar said loudly to his adjutants, "Look at these dancing beauties! They are not bad, eh?"

Upon hearing his loud and shrilled voice, all girls stopped dancing and stared angrily at Mohar.

"Ha! ha! ha!," Mohar laughed very loudly. "Continue your singing and dancing. I am the Lion of Karsog. It is your luck to perform in front of me!"

Upon hearing his name, the girls were frightened and ran away quickly, except Imla and Bimal who were brave.

"How dare you to talk like this with us? You think you can insult us just because you're stronger?" Imla said annoyingly.

"Can you be a hero by insulting girls? If you always behave like this, and didn't mend your ways then Mountain God will punish you," Bimla added.

Mohar frowned and yelled flagitiously, "Shut up! How dare you to speak with me like that!" I'll teach you both a lesson that you'll never forget."

One of his subordinates whispered to him, "Chief, they are one the most beautiful girls in the Karsog valley. Why don't you take them home as your mistresses?"

Mohar liked the idea and said, "Yes, you're right! Each one of you grab one girl. Let's go!"

The sisters were mad and their faces were flushed. They struggled hard but were unable to loosen themselves from the strong hold of the two big men. Mohar laughed at their agonies.

Suddenly there came a shout, "Leave them alone!"

Two young men appeared from behind a tree. One of them said to Mohar without the slightest fear, "Even though we two brothers are unable to match you three, we cannot let you take these girls."

Mohar said in a disdainful manner, "Then how do you think you'll free these girls from us?"

"We believe that the Mountain God will help us," said the elder one.

"You will die even before the Mountain God will come to your help," Mohar growled.

Suddenly a flash of light came down from the sky, and the clear sky became dark. The thunder rolled across the malevolent sky. The untamed power reverberated and echoed across the green woods. The thunder sound scared Mohar. One of his subordinates said to him with a trembling voice, "Chief, I think the Mountain

God is really angry? I think it's better to leave these two here."

Mohar was stunned but pretended to be undismayed. In a moment, however, he and his subordinates ran away timidly.

Once they ran away, the sky cleared up and it was pleasant weather again. The two sisters thanked two brothers for their timely help. Other girls who had ran away but watching the whole episode hiding behind trees also joined them and hailed the bravery of two brothers. They all then sang and danced happily in the woods.

Mohar however was irritated with his defeat and thinking of means to avenge his insult. He sent a messenger with an order to the girls' father, "I command you to send your two daughters to become my wives. I give you time of three days. After three days, if you didn't heed my command, I'll burn down your village and kill all people of your tribes."

The words spread like a wildfire. Everybody was worried and fearful of the repercussion. They did not like to sacrifice the two beautiful and tender girls to Mohar, but they were also afraid of his ruthless and vile anger. At last all people decided to face the consequences, but not to handover girls to the barbarian.

Three days passed. On the night of the third day, Imla and Bimla left the village quietly and walked the trail between the villages of two tribes. They knelt down and prayed respectfully to the Mountain God.

"Oh! Kind God, please protect our tribe. Do not let Mohar hurt anybody. If we have to suffer, let us two sisters take the responsibility!" they pleaded.

They prayed continuously and cried constantly. The tears drenched their clothes and the soil. It was near dawn when the first ray of sun came through the trees. Suddenly lightening flashed, followed by deafening thunder.

The Mountain God appeared and transformed Imla and Bimla into two streams, one larger than the other, which were connected together. This cut off the passage between the two villages.

The sun rose higher and the streams water became so bright that they looked like two flowing mirrors. The water flickered like two sisters blinking their beautiful eyes.

Soon, Mohar and his soldiers, all carrying machete, spears and bows and arrows, came to the streams. They were flabbergasted to see two streams.

"It's strange! Where did these two streams come from? They were not here yesterday!"

All were puzzled and conferred with each other when the two sisters suddenly emerged from the water's surface. The mountain breeze swung their black hairs and their white clothes while the water reflected the woods and their lovely figures. The elder sister said to Mohar with a firm voice, "Mohar, you have done too many bad things. If you do not repent now and mend your ways, the Mountain God will punish you and a disaster will fall upon you!"

Mohar laughed loudly, "I am the great Lion of Karsog. What can the Mountain God do to me! You two come with me quickly."

The younger sister said angrily, "Sister, he will not repent and will not change. It is useless to advise him. Let the Mountain God punish him."

After this, the two sisters, holding their hands together, vanished into the water.

Mohar shouted, "Don't you dare to escape!" and without delay jumped into the water in an attempt to catch them. As soon as he jumped into the water, a dark cloud appeared and blocked out the sky above the streams. All of a sudden, lighting flashed, thunder roared, rain poured, and a gusty wind ripped across the woods.

Mohar struggled in the water blindly. He was trying to swim desperately in the water, but the current was too swift at that time. He tried hard but at last, he became frightened and desperately staggered in all directions. But no matter where he turned, he could see neither the two sisters nor the bank. Finally losing all his strength, he drowned and his body washed away in the stream.

All his men were scared to hell and they ran away with their tail between their legs. This news soon spread all over the Karsog valley.

The villagers were much pleased at the death of Mohar, but were also sad on the disappearance of two sisters.

When night came that day, two figures came to the streams shore, murmuring the names of the two sisters. They were the two young brothers who had rescued the sisters.

"O courageous Imla and Bimla, you must feel lonesome lying there. We will accompany you and stand by your sides," they said.

For three days and three nights, they stood there. Their probity and devotion touched the Mountain God. He appeared and transformed the two brothers into two big trees with their branches tied together. They stood there forever to accompany the 'Stream Sisters'.

Since then, it is said that on nights of a full moon, the two sisters emerge from the streams and walk to the land. They sing and dance around the 'Tree Brothers' whole night, and 'Tree Brothers' sway their branches to match the rhythm of their melody.

The Magic Lake

In the land of Himachal, there was a beautiful lake surrounded by hills and mountains. The lake was so beautiful and clear that people who passed by would gasp in admiration and wonder. When the sun was high in the sky, casting the shadows of the mountain peaks across the calm expanse of water, it looked just as if there was a castle in the lake, a castle of such vast proportions that it filled the whole water. Blue water reflected the sky, as the clouds pass by. The vibrant green grass sits along the border occupied by daisies with moonlight-pale petals and a speckle of yellow in the middle. The whole surface makes a gentle, waving notion as the breeze passes by.

People of nearby villages have heard many stories about the lake. Sometimes it was said that when it is full moon and the stars gleamed like diamonds on the water, strange things could be seen rising from the clear water of lake. People with their bodies on fire and golden hairs hanging like long whips around their faces, or fiery dogs with red eyes would appear to tear the flesh from the bodies of lone travelers who walk on the beach in innocence.

Villagers have accepted that there was indeed a castle in the lake, and that the castle had a demon king. The demon king, it was said, had many servants, men who by some misfortune had fallen into the lake, or who had been captured while walking alone on its shores and were thereafter forced to remain in the service of the demon king.

In a nearby village lived a young shepherd named Neel with his evil and self-centered stepmother. His stepmother was a cruel woman; she forced him to hard work so that she could buy new clothes and eat well, while he had to be content with a few cast-off worn-out rags and the meager scraps of food his mother did not want.

One day the young shepherd was tending his herd of sheep on the side of the lake. Feeling a need for refreshment, he left his herd and made his way down to the lake shore. After he had splashed the cool water of lake onto his face, he lay back against a large rock, took out his stale *rotis*, which his stepmother had given him, and began to have his lunch.

While he was eating, Neel began to reflect upon his life. Thinking of all the cruelties he suffered from the hands of his stepmother, Neel began to cry. The tears rolled down his cheeks and sobs shook his body; he could work no harder and yet his mother wanted more and more.

As the boy began to pack away his things and set for home he saw a fish wriggling on the sand gasping for air. The fish was of dark blue color with electric blue and white rings on its body. Neel had never seen such a beautiful and brightly colored fish before. He took pity on fish and picked it and put back into lake. As soon as the fish reached the water it turned into a beautiful fairy wearing a long wavy blue gown.

Recalling the stories he had heard about the lake and the demon king, Neel began to panic, and was just starting to run away when the fairy spoke.

"Don't be afraid of me kind human!"

Neel turned to see the fairy and saw that her face was gentle and kind, and her voice was soft and melodious. He gathered some courage and walked toward the fairy, who was standing in the shallows of the lake.

The fairy said, "I was looking at you for long from the water. I'd never seen such a sad face before. In excitement of looking you from close I fell out of water. Why were you so sad and crying?"

Neel told her about his life and stepmother and how she forced him to work harder and harder.

"Come with me into the lake," the fairy said, "for the king is a kind man and may be able to help you with your problem."

The young shepherd began to feel fear well inside him once more, for he was sure that if he went into the lake he would never return. The fairy sensed the boy's fear, but in gentle tones which felt like music to the ear, she persuaded the young shepherd that he need not to fear for his life.

"I am the daughter of the king," said the fairy, "I will tell my father that how you saved me, and don't worry, you'll be safe and will return safely."

The young shepherd thought for a moment:

"What have I to lose? My mother is so cruel that even death would be better than spending the rest of my life in her bondage."

And so, throwing his fear away, Neel followed the fairy into the lake. The water was surprisingly warm than before, and the boy was amazed that he could breathe quite freely. The fairy asked the boy to close his eyes as she led the boy through the water to the castle. When they stopped and Neel opened his eyes he saw that he was standing in a large hall, elaborately decorated in gold, shining silver, and beautiful shell. At the end of the hall was a throne, and on the throne sat an old man, the king. The fairy rushed to her father and told him the whole story.

The king beckoned to the boy to come forward and as he did Neel noticed that he was not alone in the room with the fairy and the king. Standing on each side of the throne were many servants, dressed in golden and blue gowns just like the fairy who met him on the shore of the lake. When he reached the foot of the king's throne one of the servants sprang forward and placed a small chair in front of the throne for the boy to sit on. Nervously, Neel sat down and looked up into the watery blue eyes of the king.

"I've heard of all the hardship you went through in your life," said the king in a deep voice, "and I'm grateful to you for what you did to save my princess daughter."

He turned toward his group of servants and signaled one of them to come to him. The servant approached the king and bent low while the king whispered instructions into his ear. The young shepherd tried hard but could not hear what the king was saying.

The servant left the hall and returned a few moments later with a bird.

"Take this bird," said the king to the young shepherd, "it will solve all your problems, but take care that you always feed it before you feed yourself."

Neel took the bird, and with his eyes closed, the fairy led him to the shores of the lake. When he opened his eyes he was alone with the bird and the fairy was nowhere to be seen. Neel noticed that all the sheep of his herd were still grazing near the lake.

Neel went home with his herd and the bird. From that day on, everything he desired appeared before him. He would wake up in the morning and find that barley had been placed in the barley barrel, wool in the wool basket and money in the money vault. Even new clothes appeared in his clothes' drawers. He was very happy and always took great care of the bird, minding the king's instructions to always feed it before feeding himself.

Neel's mother was amazed that suddenly her son had become so wealthy, and one day she decided to go out with the herd of sheep to see if she could discover the source of infinite wealth herself. In the evening all the sheep returned home but the step-mother never returned back. Some says that she had been dragged by devil dogs into the vicious lake, but nobody saw her again.

One day Neel decided to watch the bird, for he was curious and wanted to know how the bird managed to produce the money and food and all the other necessities. Hiding himself in the house, he watched the bird as it entered the door, walked over to the hearth, and violently began shaking itself.

Suddenly, the bird's feathers fell to the ground, revealing a beautiful woman, the most beautiful woman Neel had ever seen. The woman went to the barley barrel, opened the lid, and placed in it the barley, which appeared from nowhere. Then she did the same with the wool basket, the money vault, going all around the house producing everything that the young shepherd needed.

Neel couldn't contain himself any longer. He collected the bird's feathers from the ground, and as soon as he picked the last feather, all feathers burst into a flame. The beautiful woman appeared from nowhere in front of him and started wailing:

"What have you done? Now I'll never be able to return to my original form," said the woman.

I'm extremely sorry! I was just curious to know how you manage to do all this. I never thought that it will end like this," Neel said in a trembling voice.

"Now I'll never be able to return to my kingdom, and will have to live in human form forever," cried the woman.

Neel consoled her and promised that he will marry her and will give her even more care and love. But soon Neel was frightened of thought that the chief of his village would see his beautiful wife and snatch her to make his own wife. Fearing this Neel covered her face with black soot to hide her beauty, and kept her in the house away from the eyes of the people.

As time passed, the young shepherd grew very rich, and with his wealth he grew exceedingly bold.

"Why do I worry," he thought, "I have more money than chief, and he will not dare to steal the woman from me, for I can buy weapons and men and become stronger than him."

Thinking this, Neel washed the soot from his wife's face and took her into town to show her to the people, for he was very proud of her beauty.

The chief was also in the town and he saw the woman. He had never seen such beauty before and he was determined that she should become his wife, and sent his men to fetch the woman to him. The young shepherd was distressed and called upon the men of the town to help him, but they were too afraid of the chief, and not one man would come forward to help Neel save his wife.

Feeling very sad, the young shepherd went down to the shore of the lake, sat down by the large rock and began to cry. Just as before, the fairy appeared.

"Why are you crying this time?" she asked.

"I have lost my wife," the boy replied, and told the whole story of how he picked the feathers and they burned and kept the beautiful woman hidden from the eyes of the people by covering her face in soot, but growing bold he washed her face, showing her beauty to the people, and so lost her forever to the chief.

The fairy asked Neel to follow her into the lake again, for the king needed to be told the story.

"Perhaps," said the fairy, "the king may be able to help you again."

The young shepherd soon found himself in front of the throne once more at the feet of the king of the lake. After he heard the story of how Neel had lost the beautiful woman, the king gave him a small wooden box.

"Take this box," the king said, holding it out to the young shepherd. "Now" the king continued, "go to the top of a high hill and call the chief to fight. When he has assembled his people at the base of the hill, open the box and shout 'Fight!'"

Neel took the box and thanked the king. The fairy led him to the shore of lake and bid goodbye.

The young shepherd climbed the high hill and after reaching the top challenged the chief for fight. The chief gathered his men and reached at the base of hill.

Neel opened the box and shouted "Fight!". Hundreds of men charged out of the box and defeated the chief's men.

Neel won back his beautiful wife. He also took half of the chief's lands and became a rich, benevolent leader of the people. The young shepherd also returned the box to the king of the lake, thanking him and lived in peace and happiness for all of his life.

Sound of Snowstorm

Once upon a time, there lived a man named Moti with his father. Moti's mother died when he was a young kid. His father brought him up with utmost love and care. His father was a woodcutter, and Moti used to help him in cutting woods. When Moti grew up to become a young lad his father married him to a beautiful girl who gave him two lovely children. Soon his wife died while giving birth to the second child.

As winter came, the mountains became covered deep with snow. One day when Moti and his father were returning from jungle they got caught in a snowstorm. They kept on walking in the snowstorm, but it was becoming very difficult to find the path.

"Moti, I think we'll not be able to reach home in such a snow. There is a cave nearby, we should try to reach there and seek shelter," said father.

They changed their course and reached a small mountain cave. They decided to wait until the snowstorm passed.

They entered the cave and lit a fire with the woods they had cut. As they were warming their cold bodies, father said: "Tonight, we should stay here. If we go out, we would surely die."

Ok, father! said Moti, I'll make a temporary curtain from pine leaves and branches to cover the mouth of cave.

After covering the mouth of cave, they felt a much relieved as now snow and wind were not entering the cave. Then they both sat down and started making preparation to sleep.

"Moti, why don't you get remarried?" said father, "I'm now getting old and want to see you with a wife and my grandchildren with a mother before I die."

Moti was still in love with his dead wife so he used to avoid the talks of remarriage, so he didn't say any word, and went to sleep. Just after midnight Moti woke up from his sleep. He felt like that the air has become too cold. He got up to check the curtain. The cold wind was blowing very fast, suddenly he noticed a figure standing near the mouth of cave. Moti became frightened, he ran back to his father, who was fast asleep. Soon Moti realized that wind has stopped and it's again warm in the cave. He gathered himself and went back to sleep.

Next morning when they woke up, the sky was clear. They headed towards their home. That day the father fell sick. He caught cold on the night they spend in cave. Next day Moti went alone to jungle for cutting wood. When he was returning home, though it was a clear sky, a snowstorm started out of nowhere and soon he was almost knee-deep in the snow. He thought of the cave and head toward it as fast as he could. Many hours passed but the snow was still falling. Moti decided to spend the night in cave. After few hours, Moti woke up because he was feeling very cold. He saw that woods have all been burned up and the curtain was opened and snow was coming through the mouth of cave. Suddenly he saw someone in the snowstorm near the mouth of cave. It was a woman who had beautiful white face like snow. Moti was surprised to see such beautiful woman alone in jungle. She came inside the cave and sat down near him. Moti was held spell bounded. He could feel the breath of woman. It was very cold. Moti felt shivers running down his spine. Suddenly he felt very weak, and he thought he was going to die and hallucinating.

"Please help me," he said.

When she saw his eyes, suddenly her cold expression became gentle.

"You are very young and have beautiful eyes. I will save you, but you must not tell anyone that you met me and I saved you."

"Ok," Moti answered while trembling.

"Close your eyes, and hold my hands," she said.

Moti did as she said, and after some time when he opened his eyes he found himself standing in front of his home. Moti was very confused; he couldn't decide whether what just happened with him was a dream or a reality. He decided not to tell anyone, not even to his father, about this incident.

One year passed, and Moti never told anyone about that incident. Moti's father had passed away of illness. He never could recover from his illness.

Winters came again. It was a rainy day. Moti couldn't go to his work due to inclement weather. He was standing near the window of his house. He saw a woman standing in front of his house waiting for the rain to stop. He felt sorry for her because she was all drenched and shivering in cold. He was a kind man, so he invited her to his house. Her name was Mala. She was very beautiful. He was fascinated by her beauty, and she, too, since he was kind. Soon they fell in love with each other and got married. Mala turned out to be a great wife and great mother to Moti's children.

Nine years passed and they were leading a very happy and satisfied life. But there was one thing Moti was worried about: every time Mala was exposed to the sunshine she got sick. So he always took good care of her.

One snowy night, as he was watching Mala sew his coat he remembered that he had seen a beautiful woman who looked like her in the past.

"I had seen a beautiful woman like you a long time ago," he said.

"Who? What like?" she asked.

"It was a snowy night like tonight. I saw a snow woman."

Mala stood up and said, "You told it finally."

Moti was startled. "You are …?"

Mala turned around and changed her form. It was the snow woman Moti had met that day at the cave.

"I wanted to live happily with you forever. Why did you break our promise? I will have to go now and will not see you again. Good bye."

After saying this, she left their house. Moti tried to stop her, but he could not. As soon as she went out of the house, she vanished in the thin air. He and his children were just sitting there in the snowstorm helpless.

After this incidence, Moti became very depressed. He was not able to sleep well, and was physically and emotionally tormented. He always cursed himself for breaking the promise and letting her beautiful wife go.

One day a *sadhu* passed through his village. He saw sad Moti sitting on porch of his house.

"Will you please give me some food to eat?" *sadhu* asked.

"Yes, please come inside," Moti said.

Moti offered him some food to eat. While eating *sadhu* asked, "Why are you so sad? And where is your wife? I noticed that you made food yourself."

Moti told him the whole story. *Sadhu* heard the story patiently and said, "Son you and your children are very lucky, the woman you married was a snow witch. She has to suck life nectar of one human being after every ten years to keep herself warm. Your father didn't die of old age or illness. That witch had sucked his life nectar while you were sleeping that night in the cave. That night she had come with the intention of killing you. But she found you so handsome and got attracted to you that she had no option but to spare you, and kill your father instead."

"It was tenth year, and if you'd not broken the promise, she would have killed one of your children," *sadhu* continued.

Moti was surprised and taken aback. I couldn't believe that he was living with a witch this whole time. He thanked the *sadhu* for unfurling the mystery of his father's death and the truth behind his wife's sudden departure.

From that day on, nobody ventures out in snowstorm. When we go to snowy mountains, we can hear the screeching sound of snowstorm. It is the snow witch crying. She wanders and looks for a warm hearted human to help her cold body keep warm.

∞ ∞ ∞

The Gold Mountain

Once upon a time there was a poor but brave and intelligent young man named Khem. He was very hardworking and obedient to his parents. He used to work as a porter with a merchant, but the merchant was so miser that he never paid full wager to Khem. What Khem earned was not sufficient to meet the both ends. So one day he decided to go to city and try his luck.

He took a shovel and went to the market place of city to see if perchance somebody would hire him as a worker. The sun was about to set when a rich, proud merchant came along in a gilded carriage. All other workers at the market place, as soon as they see him, rushed away and hid themselves in the corners. Only Khem remained as he was in dire need of work and he had nowhere to go.

"Are you looking for work, young man?" the very rich merchant said to him.

"Yes, that's what I came here for," replied Khem.

"And your price?"

"A hundred gold coins for a day will be sufficient for me."

"Why so much?"

"If too much, go and look for someone else, plenty of people were around and when they saw you coming, all of them rushed away."

"All right, tomorrow come to the horse stable downhill," said merchant.

The next day, early in the morning, Khem arrived at the horse stable; the very rich merchant was already there waiting. They took two horses and set away. For quite a long time they journeyed, and finally they reached a town. That town was surrounded by high mountains, and near one end of town something seemed to be in flames.

"There seems something is on fire," said Khem.

"No, it is my golden palace," said the merchant.

When they reached the golden palace the rich merchant's wife and their young daughter, a lovely girl, prettier than you could think or even dream of, greet them. The family met and went to the palace. And along with them went their new workman. They sat around the dining table and ate and drank and were cheerful.

"One day does not count," the rich merchant said, "let us have a good time and leave work for tomorrow."

The young Khem was a fine, brave fellow, handsome and stately, and the merchant's lovely daughter liked him well. She left the room and made him a sign to follow her. Then she gave him two stones.

"Take them," she said, "when you'll be in any trouble, these will be useful."

The next day the rich merchant with his hired workman went to the high golden mountain. The young fellow saw at once that there was no use trying to climb or even to crawl up.

"Well," said the merchant, "let us have a drink for courage."

And he gave Khem some drowsy drink. Khem drank the glass and fell asleep. The rich merchant took out a sharp knife, killed a wretched horse, cut it open, put the fellow inside, pushed in the shovel, and sewed the horse's skin together, and himself sat down in the bushes. All at once crows came flying, black crows with iron beaks. They took hold of the carcass, lifted it up to the top of the high mountain, and began to pick at it. The crows soon ate up the horse and were about to begin on Khem, when he woke up, pushed away the crows, looked around and asked out loud:

"Where am I?"

The rich merchant below answered:

"On a golden mountain; don't waste time, take the shovel and dig for gold."

And the young man dug and dug, and all the gold he dug he

threw down, and the rich merchant loaded it upon the carts.

"Enough!" finally shouted the master, "Thanks for your help, Farewell!"

"And I, how shall I get down?"

"As you like, there have already perished ninety-nine of such fellows as you. With you the count will be rounded and you will be the hundredth."

The proud, rich merchant was off.

"What shall I do?" thought the poor boy, "it is impossible to get down! But to stay here means certain death, a cruel death from hunger."

He stood upon the mountain, while above the black crows were circling, the black crows with iron beaks, as if feeling already the prey. The fellow tried to think how it all happened, and he remembered the lovely girl and what she said to him in giving him two stones. He remembered how she said:

"*Take them, when you'll be in any trouble, these will be useful.*"

"I fancy she had something in mind, let us try."

Khem took out the stones and struck them with each other and lo! two *djinns* were standing before him.

"What is your wish? What are your commands?" said they.

"Take me down from this mountain," ordered Khem.

And at once the two took hold of him and carefully brought him down. Khem walks along the road from where they had came, and finally reach the city market. After some days Khem took again his shovel and went to the market place in search of work. The same very rich merchant came along in his gilded carriage, and, as before, all other workers who saw him coming rushed away. But Khem remained there. Merchant was surprised to see him, but as there was no other workman he said:

"Will you be my workman?"

"I will at two hundred gold coins a day. If so, let us to work."

"A rather expensive fellow, eh?"

"If too expensive go to others; get a cheap man. There were plenty of people, but you can see not one is left now," replied Khem.

"Well, all right. Come tomorrow to the horse stable downhill."

They met at the same place, took horses and started their journey. The first day they spent in celebration, and on the second, master and workman went to work. When they reached the golden mountain the rich, proud merchant treated his hired man to a tumbler.

"Before all, have a drink."

"Wait! You are the master, you must drink first. Let me serve you this time."

The young man had already prepared some of the intoxicating stuff and he quickly mixed it with the wine and presented it to the master. The proud merchant drank and fell sound asleep. Khem killed a miserable old horse, cut it open, pushed his master and the shovel inside, sewed it all up and hid himself in the bushes. All at once black crows came flying, black crows with iron beaks; they promptly lifted up the horse with the sleeping merchant inside, bore it to the top of the mountain, and began to pick the bones of their prey. When the merchant awoke he looked here and there and looked everywhere.

"Where am I?" he asked.

"Upon the golden mountain. Now do not waste time, take the shovel and dig. Dig quickly and I'll teach you how to come down."

The proud, rich merchant had to obey and dug and dug. Twelve big carts of gold were loaded.

"Enough!" shouted Khem, "Thank you, and farewell!"

"And I?"

"There are already ninety-nine fellows perished there, with you there will be a hundred."

Khem took along with him the twelve heavy carts with gold, and arrived at the golden palace. He told the whole story to merchant's daughter. The daughter was initially in grief for his father, but knowing that he was a bad person and would have to meet same fate one day, she accepted the proposal of marriage of Khem. She also became mistress of all her father's wealth, and Khem with his family moved to a large town to live.

And the rich merchant, the proud, rich merchant? He himself, like his many victims, became the prey of the black crows, black crows with iron beaks.

Well, it's not always happy ending for everyone.

The Betrayal

A long time ago the rooster and the peacock were best friends. They used to hang out together and spend the whole day in plays and recreations. In those times, the rooster used to have the colorful feathered tail and astonishingly beautiful crest (crown) which we see today in the peacock. The peacock was an ugly looking bird with large body, fallen crest, ugly feet and short dull tail.

The rooster used to proudly flaunt his crest and feathers and he was apple of eyes of all other animals and birds. He was treated as a beautiful prince by all. Females quarreled and ach their necks in their efforts to steal a glance of the most beautiful bird on the planet. Peacock was very proud on the beauty of his friend and proud to be his friend as well. But somewhere deep in his heart he used to long for such beauty for himself. He used to think that he is tall and bigger than the rooster and such colorful feathers and beautiful crest will suit him more.

Female birds followed the rooster like the rats and children of Hamelin followed the Pied Piper. But the peacock never could command even half the attention of the females that the rooster could hands down. He went to bed every night with the hope of getting out of bed as beautiful as the rooster the next morning. But that never happened. He woke up as the same ugly peacock every day.

The rooster could see his predicament, and he always wished to help the peacock. But god had made them as they were.

Then came the week of annual celebrations. During this week

all animals and birds meet at the square donning their best attires and possessions. Games were played and music and celebrations were everywhere. This was the darkest week for peacock. He shut himself to his house, and was feeling very lonely that suddenly he heard a knock on his doors. It was the rooster, his friend.

"Let's go to square and enjoy!" said the rooster.

"I'm not feeling like going," replied the peacock.

"What's wrong my friend, why are you so sad?" asked the rooster.

"People make fun of me, they say I'm ugly, my head is so blunt and my tail is so short!"

The rooster always loved the peacock and wanted to see him happy. So he decided to lend his crest and tail to peacock for one day.

"Here my friend, take my crest and tail for today. But please promise me that you'll take good care of my crest, it's my most valuable possession," requested the rooster.

The peacock was overjoyed hearing this and promised to take care of crest and return it and tail before dawn.

That day, the rooster didn't dare to venture out of his room. He remained indoors. He thought it quite an embarrassment to go in public without his most coveted possessions.

But when the peacock reached the square all attention shifted to him. Females considered him even more beautiful than the rooster. They never realized that he was the same peacock in someone else's attire. Peacock spent the whole day and night in merry making and enjoying the celebrations. He sang and dance and made many new friends. Just before the dawn the sky became overcast with clouds, and heavy downpour started. All animals were enjoying the rain, and dancing. But the peacock was worried for the crest. He feared that the rain will spoil the crest, and how will he face the rooster with spoiled crest.

To protect the crest from rain, he spread the feathers of his tail. Seeing this all animals were enchanted and enthralled with the majestic view of colorful feathers. They had never seen such brilliant plumage on the tail marked with iridescent eyes, with a spectrum of blue, gold, orange, yellow and purple colors. The peacock himself was so thrilled that he couldn't speak a word. He was spell bounded with the beauty that his tail has bestowed to him. He wished to look the same for eternity. At that moment he decided to keep the tail for himself, and betray his best friend. But he also had the crest of rooster, and if he go back to return the crest he'll have to return the tail as well. So, finally, he decided not to return back to rooster at all.

Poor rooster waited and waited for his friend peacock. But the peacock never came back or returned his crest and tail. Soon the first light of sun appeared on horizon. But there was no sign of peacock. In anger and disgust, the rooster screamed and shouted. He called out to peacock at the top of his voice to return his crest and tail, over and over again. But the peacock never returned.

So when you hear the rooster's clarion at the sunrise, it is because he is screaming at the top of his voice, asking peacock, the Cheat, to return his prized possessions.

And likewise when you see peacock spreading feathers of his tail, just as the clouds gather and it is time for a downpour, he is not dancing, but protecting his crest from rain.

Dogs' Wagging Tails

There lived a farmer in a remote hill village. He owned a dog and a cat, both of which were very obedient and very useful to the farmer. The dog had served his master for many years and had become so old that he had lost his teeth and was unable to fight any more, but he was a good and alert guide and companion to the cat who was strong and cunning.

The master had a daughter who was married at another village some distance from home, and very often he sent the dog and the cat with presents to the daughter.

One day he called the faithful animals and made them carry a diamond ring to his daughter.

"You are strong and young," he said to the cat, "You may carry the ring, but you must be careful not to drop it."

And to the dog he said: "You must accompany the cat to guide her and save her from harm."

They promised to do their best, and started out. All went well until they came to a river. As there was neither bridge nor boat, there was no way to cross but to swim.

"Let me take the diamond ring," said the dog as they were about to plunge into the water.

"Oh, no," replied the cat, "the master gave it to me to carry."

"But you cannot swim well," argued the dog, "I am strong and can take good care of it."

But the cat refused to give up the ring until finally the dog threatened to kill her, and then she reluctantly gave it to him.

The river was wide and the water so swift that they grew

very tired, and just before they reached the opposite bank the dog dropped the ring. They searched carefully, but could not find it anywhere, and after a while they turned back to tell their master of the sad loss. Just before reaching the house, however, the dog was so overcome with fear that he turned and ran away and never was seen again.

The cat went on alone, and when the master saw her coming he called out to know why she had returned so soon and what had become of her companion. The poor cat was frightened, but she explained how the ring had been lost and how the dog had run away.

On hearing her story the master was very angry, and commanded that all his people should search for the dog, and that it should be punished by having its tail cut off.

He also ordered that all the dogs in the world should join in the search, and ever since when one dog meets another he says:

"Are you the old dog that lost the diamond ring? If so, your tail must be cut off."

Then immediately each shows his teeth and sign 'no' by wagging their tails to prove that they are not the guilty one.

Since then, too, cats have been afraid of water and will not swim across a river if they can avoid it.

The Squirrel Wife

Once upon a time there was a rich merchant who was married to a beautiful lady. They were living a happy and prosperous life but with one void; they had no child. So the wife made a great pet of a young squirrel, and fed it every day.

The relatives of merchant advised him to remarry so that his business can have an heir. The merchant told his decision to his wife who was very upset of the thought of her husband's second marriage. One day it entered her head to deceive the merchant, so she told him that, she is going on hills to seek blessings of a divine *sadhu* for child. The husband agreed and the wife with her faithful servants set out to hills. Some days later she returned with an apple. When the husband enquired about the apple the wife told him that the divine *sadhu* had given that apple to her and after eating it she will bore a child.

Some days later the wife announced the merchant that before the end of the year, an heir would be born. She pretended to be pregnant for months and on the appointed day she sent her own nurse (whom she had bribed) to tell the merchant that the child was born, and was a daughter. The merchant hastened to see the young child, who was, in reality, no child, but the tame squirrel. The wife persuaded the merchant that the *sadhu* had pointed out that the husband must not look on face of child for sixteen years, for, if she looked at him, he would die, and, if he looked at her, she would die. The poor merchant had no choice but to agree, and thus the wife kept up her deception for sixteen years, and hid her pet squirrel from everybody.

At last, when the sixteen years were over, she said one day to the merchant:

"Last night the divine *sadhu* came to my dream and told me that you should not look upon your daughter's face till she is married, lest evil come upon her, so go and make arrangements to marry her to a suitor of good family."

So they sent their family priest to seek for a husband for their daughter; and he went from place to place, until he came to a city where there was another rich merchant who had five sons, all of whom were married but the youngest, whose name was Kunwar; so the priest chose him, and all was prepared for the marriage.

There was a great feast held, and great rejoicings daily took place in the merchant's house. When at last the palanquin came, for the bride to be carried to her home, the wife hid the squirrel inside it, and nobody guessed that there was, in reality, no bride. The wife also instructed the groom's family that only groom can have the first sight of the bride, so take the palanquin direct to the room of groom. If anybody saw her before the groom it will be bad omen.

On reaching his home the young bridegroom had the palanquin placed at the door of his room, so that none might see his bride enter; and great indeed was his surprise, when he looked inside, to find nobody there but a squirrel.

For very shame he held his peace, and told nobody of it, but gave orders in the house that he and his wife would live apart by themselves; and she would be in such strict veil, that even the women of the household would not be allowed to visit her. This gave great offence to everybody; but they put it down to his jealousy, owing to his wife's great beauty, and obeyed.

At last his other brother's wife rebelled, and said:

"We should we do all the household work; your wife must also take her share in it."

Kunwar was now very sad, for he felt the time had come for his secret to be discovered, and he would become the laughing stock of the whole family. The squirrel, who was a great favorite of his, noticed his sadness, and asked him the cause of it.

"Why are you sad, O husband?"

"I am sad because they say you must do some of the household work; and how will you do it, being only a squirrel?"

"What is it they want me to do?" asked the squirrel.

"To mop the floor," replied Kunwar.

"Well, tell them to do their own portion of the work, and leave me to do mine at my leisure," said the squirrel.

This was done, and at night the squirrel went and dipped her tail into the water, and soon had the room better done than the others. In the morning all the family was surprised to see the clever way in which Kunwar's wife had done her work, and they said:

"No wonder you hide your wife, when she is so clever and competent."

The next day the task was to grind some wheat, and again Kunwar's heart was heavy, for how could a squirrel turn a heavy stone handmill, and grind wheat? But the squirrel said as before:

"Tell them to do their work, and to leave mine alone. I will do it when I'll wish."

When night came, she went into the room, and with her sharp little teeth grind the wheat to powder. Kunwar was very pleased with her, and so were they all, and nothing more was said until the next day, when the allotted task was to cook *gajar halwa*.

The poor little squirrel was indeed at her wits' end how to perform the task, for how could so small an animal make so difficult a dish? She tried, and she tried, but failed each time in her attempts, until it was nearly morning.

The squirrel was so embarrassed with failure that it determined to go to the river and there drown itself; yet when it tried to do so, its courage failed. So it alternately threw itself into the water and then changed mind and came out again. Its conduct attracted the attention of an old parrot couple, who had their nest nearby.

'I wonder what that squirrel is doing?" said the male.

"Let's call it and ask," said the female.

They called the squirrel and asked the reason of its strange conduct. The squirrel told them everything, and when it had done the parrot said:

"We'll help you but in return you'll also have to do a favor for us."

"What can a timid squirrel like me do for you?" said the squirrel.

"Near this place behind those bushes is a small pond surrounded by fruit trees. We both are very old so we cannot eat raw fruits from the trees. Instead we used to pick the ripe fruits which had fallen on the ground. Few days back a crocodile came to that pond to dwell, and whenever we go there to pick fruits it charges on us to kill. If you'll bring some fruits for us then we'll help you."

The squirrel reached the pond and started picking fallen fruits that suddenly the crocodile came charging toward it. The squirrel ran for its life, but the crocodile caught its tail in his teeth. The squirrel was writhing in pain but didn't lose its cool and said to crocodile:

"Why do you trouble other animals and chevy them?"

"It makes me happy," the crocodile replied.

"So if you're happy holding me with my tail then why don't you laugh?" said the squirrel.

So the crocodile said "Ha! Ha! Ha!", and in order to say it, had to open his mouth, the squirrel escaped and quickly placed a long stick between his open jaws. The crocodile's mouth got stuck and it pleaded the squirrel to remove the stick.

"I'll remove the stick but you'll have to promise that you'll not harass other animals who came here to drink water and pick fallen fruits," said the squirrel.

"Ok, I promise," said the crocodile in pain.

The squirrel removed the stick and the crocodile silently get away from there. The squirrel picked some fruits and returned back to the parrot couple, and told them that the crocodile will not be any more a problem for them.

The parrot couple thanked the squirrel and chanted a *mantra*, and then blew on squirrel, which forthwith turned into a most beautiful girl. She thanked the parrots and quickly returned to her home, and resumed finishing her task. Just before the dawn she finished making the *gajar halwa*.

When other members of the family awoke, and came in, they were greatly amazed at her beauty, and led her by the hand to their own rooms. Meantime, Kunwar, her husband, was stricken with grief, thinking his poor little squirrel had left him. He sought her everywhere, and when he could not find her, began to cry:

"O my squirrel, my squirrel, where are you?"

The women standing there scolded him for this, and said:

"Why do you call your beautiful wife a squirrel? She is not dead, but has at last been found by us, and is with the other ladies in the home."

But Kunwar, who knew nothing of what had happened, only wept the more, for he thought they were making fun of him, so he went to his own room, where he flung himself on his bed, and continued to weep.

At last he looked up and saw, standing beside him, a beautiful girl, who said:

"Do not weep, O husband, for I am your squirrel."

Then she told him all that had happened. This was indeed good news, and it was not long before the grateful squirrel wrote to her foster-mother, who had been so good and kind to her when she was only a helpless little creature, and invited her and her father to come on a visit. This was the first time the merchant had seen or touched his daughter, and he was indeed pleased to find she was so beautiful. So there were great rejoicings everywhere, and they all lived happily ever after.

Hungry Ghost

In a hill village of Himachal there lived a young man named Guri. He was a small-time trader and made a satisfactory living for himself and his family. He was very simpleton and naïve. He was so simpleton that the smallest day-to-day problems made him worried. And when he was worried, he ran to his friend Ranji for guidance. Ranji was the sole barber of the village. Every day he sat under a mango tree with his chair, mirror and tools, waiting for people to come along and shave their beards or heads.

One day a distant relative of Guri's wife came to his house and informed him that his in-laws have invited him to their place. Hearing this Guri immediately became nervous, and he started feeling butterflies in his stomach.

In such rural parts of the region, a young man always feels shy and nervous when going to his in-laws' place for the first time. He immediately thought of Ranji and rushed to seek his help. Ranji was busy shaving the beard of a customer, sitting under the tree, when Guri came running and panting. He was looking more nervous than ever. Ranji knows that Guri's troubles were nothing but a hick-up or two. He knows that everything will soon be back to normal and there is nothing to be alarmed about, so at the sight of him he laughed and asked jokingly whether some sky has fallen on him. But Guri was really worried because he had to go to his in-law's place. At this Ranji laughed again and said:

"You're a lucky man, you should be happy! Your in-laws will treat you like a king when you will reach there. They will run around you to look after all your needs."

"Stop pulling my leg Ranji," said Guri irritatingly, "I'm scared, I never went alone to my in-laws's house."

"Don't be so wimp! You'll be alright there. You're not alone, your wife will be there on your side," said Ranji.

Guri told him that his wife would not be accompanying him. So he was all alone and he did not know what to say there, and what to do there. On hearing this Ranji assured his friend that he will teach him how to behave at his in-laws.

"Why don't you come with me my friend?" Guri suggested.

"Me? What will I do there? That's your in-laws place and I'll be unwanted there," said Ranji.

Guri insisted and pleaded to Ranji to come along with him. At last Ranji agreed to accompany his friend. Next morning they sport their best attires and wore colorful turbans and set out to reach in-laws' village. On the way Ranji told Guri:

"You must remember two things. First, don't behave like a jabberer and second don't eat too much."

"But how will I know that what to say or do and when," asked Guri innocently.

"Hmm…!" Ranji thought for a moment and said, "If I hem once, that means 'no' and you'll stop talking or doing anything, and if I hem twice, that means 'yes', and you can do or say what you please, got it?"

"Ok," said Guri confusingly.

In a few hours they arrived at Guri's in-laws house. The whole family turned out to welcome them. Guri's in-laws greeted them with folded hands, and asked about their journey. Guri was about to open his mouth and tell them about their journey that suddenly he remembered what Ranji had told him about not to talk too much. So he returned his in-laws' greeting with folded hands only and said not a single word.

Ranji spoke instead and said that Guri was tired after a long journey and he requires rest. Soon they were led to the kitchen for dinner. They sat on comfy cushions which were spread on the floor. Guri's eyes almost popped out of his head to see the food, particularly the crisp and delicious *pooris*. He ate a whole *poori* in one morsel when suddenly he heard Ranji hemming loudly. He looked at Ranji, who signaled him to break the poori in two halves by raising his two fingers. Imbecile Guri thought that Ranji wishes him to finish his dinner early and asking him to eat two *poories* at once. As soon as he picked two *poories* Ranji hemmed again, this time more loudly.

Guri simply had to follow his friend's advice. So, after the second *poori*, he refused everything else that was offered. His in-laws kept insisting him to eat more but with heavy heart he kept saying no. Meanwhile Ranji was eating away steadily, enjoying every dish that was decorated in the platter. Guri could only see Ranji devour all dishes that were specially prepared for him.

After the dinner was over, the two friends were led to a room to sleep. The mattresses were so comfortable that the moment they lay down, they fell asleep.

But in the middle of the night Guri woke up. His stomach was making the funniest sounds, rumbling and gurgling. He was feeling very hungry and he was not able to sleep anymore. Guri lay still for some time, hoping he would fall asleep, but he soon realized that it was hopeless. With each passing moment he got hungrier. At last he could stand it no more. He shook Ranji and tried to wake him up, but he was sleeping like a log. Furious Guri kicked him so hard that poor Ranji almost fell off his bed.

"What's your problem," asked Ranji irritatingly.

"I'm starving here of hunger and you're sleeping like a prince and that too at MY IN-LAWS' HOUSE?" said Guri furiously.

"But what can we do? Everybody is sleeping around here. We cannot just wake them up and say that you're feeling hungry. They'll think that their son-in-law is a glutton," Ranji tried to convince Guri.

But it was impossible for Guri to stand hunger anymore, so he pleaded Ranji to find some means to feed him. Ranji rolled out of his bed and opened the door and peeped out. In front of their room was a courtyard, and on the other side of the courtyard was a room. Ranji recalled that Guri's mother-in-law had brought a can of *ghee* from that room, so probably that room is the kitchen of the house.

"Come, I think I found the kitchen, we surely will get something to eat from there," said Ranji.

Guri was overjoyed to hear this, but this joy was momentarily as the door of kitchen was secured with a big lock.

"At this hour of night we will not get any food until we wake up your mother-in-law," said Ranji.

But out of shyness Guri refused to do so. In that case Ranji proposed that they should go back to sleep and wait till morning. But Guri was not able to control the fire in his stomach and pleaded again to Ranji to do something.

"Now there is only one option," said Ranji.

"And what's that?" asked Guri. "I'll do anything for just one bite of food."

"We've to sneak into the kitchen from the roof. If we are lucky enough we would definitely find something to eat," Ranji suggested.

They both quickly climbed on the roof of the kitchen. Ranji removed few slates from the top of roof and made enough space for Guri to sneak in. Then they both tied their turbans and made a rope so that Guri can climb down from it. Guri entered the kitchen, while his friend was standing on roof in guard.

"Don't forget to haul me up when I pull the turban," said Guri.

"Ok, I'll wait here for you," assured Ranji.

Guri climb down the rope and reached the kitchen. It was pitch dark in there and Guri was not able to see a thing. But slowly, as his eyes got used to the dark, he could see some utensils, tins, bottles and buckets. There were sacks of rice and wheat but nothing else that he could eat. And then Guri caught sight of an earthen pitcher hanging with a rope from the roof. His heart leapt up. He knew it contained something to be eaten.

Guri dragged a box to stand up on it and stretched out one arm as far as it would go. But he barely managed to touch the bottom of the pitcher. He picked up a stick standing in a corner and gave the pitcher a smart tap. Nothing happened, so he tapped once again, this time forcefully. There was a cracking sound and a thin stream of something began to flow out of the pitcher. Guri eagerly opened his mouth to catch the stream, took a big gulp and realized it was honey.

For a few minutes Guri stood under the pitcher and drank his fill of honey. But suddenly, without warning, a large chunk of the pitcher broke away and all content of pitcher came pouring down upon him. Before Guri had time to get off the box, he was surfeited with honey and smeared with it from head to toe. It was all over his face and hair. It got into his eyes and ears and ran down his neck into his shirt. He tried to get away but there was honey under his feet and he slipped on the floor. He pulled the turban to signal his friend to haul him up, but Ranji was nowhere to be seen. Ranji was so tired that he felt asleep on the roof.

Guri tried every possible method to haul him up but failed. He was now feeling tired himself and decided to take a short rest before trying again to get out of kitchen. In dark he touched something soft and cozy and sat there. Eventually he fell fast asleep there. The soft thing on which he was sleeping was wool. The wool stuck fast to the honey, and covered his body and his hands, so that he looked more like a sheep than a man.

That night some thieves broke into the house. They saw the lock on the kitchen door and thought that something valuable is locked in it. They opened the lock with master key and entered the kitchen. In the darkness they tripped on the Guri who was fast asleep, and they thought he was a very fine and fat sheep; so they put him into a bag and ran away, taking him with them. After a short distance Guri woke up and found himself in a bag. He shouted: "Let me go, let me go." This frightened the robbers, who had never heard a sheep call out before, and so they put down the bag.

"What is it? Is it some kind of magic?" asked one robber.

"I think there is a ghost in this bag," said another.

Guri, who was hearing all this, understood that he has been kidnapped, and if he said any more word then robbers will know that he is an ordinary man and they will kill him. Out of fear he didn't said any word.

The robbers decided that they will leave the sheep from where they'd picked it. Once again they broke into the house and left Guri in the kitchen and locked the door.

Ranji, who was awake by now, was desperately calling his friend from the roof. Guri released himself from the bag and caught hold of rope which Ranji was pulling. But this was easier said than done. Ranji was a thin, skinny fellow and Guri was no lightweight. Besides, the honey had made Guri's hand slippery and wool has made him heavier. Ranji pulled for all he was worth. But he barely managed to lift Guri a couple of feet off the ground before he ran out of breath. And back went Guri with a loud thud.

The noise woke up Guri's in-laws and they came running. At the very sight of them Ranji's heart sank. But he kept his composure and told them a story to save the situation. He said that for the last two years a ghost has been after him, and the ghost has followed him to their house and that he needs to be alone to throw it out. Otherwise the ghost may very well take a liking to one of them and never leave.

Guri's mother-in-law quickly handed over the key and the two of them hurried back to their room. Ranji opened the store and told Guri to come out. Covered with wool and dripping with honey, Guri came out. From a chink in their door his in-laws were watching. When they saw Guri covered with cotton, they thought that it is the ghost. They clutched at each other for sheer fright, ducked their heads and stayed there.

Now the coast was clear. Ranji took Guri to a tube well behind the house. Guri had a bath and buried his sticky clothes in a field nearby. Next morning when he got up from bed he acted completely innocent and clean. Once again he ate little for the morning meal. But on the way back, at the next village, he and Ranji had a good feed of milk and *jalebis*. And then the two friends went back home, laughing all the way.

9 798431 241970